For Dr Sharma

First published 1983 by
Walker Books Ltd
184-192 Drummond Street
London NW1 3HP

© 1983 Helen Oxenbury

First printed 1983
Reprinted 1986
Printed and bound by
L.E.G.O., Vicenza, Italy

British Library Cataloguing in Publication Data
Oxenbury, Helen
The check-up. — (First picture books)
I. Title   II. Series
823'.914[J]   PZ7

ISBN 0-7445-0038-9

The Check-up

Helen Oxenbury

WALKER BOOKS
LONDON

Mum took me to the doctor
for a check-up.
'You'll have to wait your
turn,' the nurse said.
The waiting room smelt funny.
I opened the window.

Nobody wanted to talk to me.
'Perhaps they're not feeling
well,' Mum whispered.

'Who's next?' the doctor said.
'Come on, it's our turn,' Mum said.
'I want to go home,' I said.

'Well, young man, shall we have
a listen to your chest?'
I sat on Mum's lap.
'Look,' Mum said. 'It doesn't hurt.'

'If you do what the doctor says,'
Mum whispered, 'I'll buy you
a little something on the way home.'

'Let's go home now, Mum,' I said.
The doctor fell off his chair.

'Call the nurse,' said the doctor.
'I'm so sorry,' said Mum.

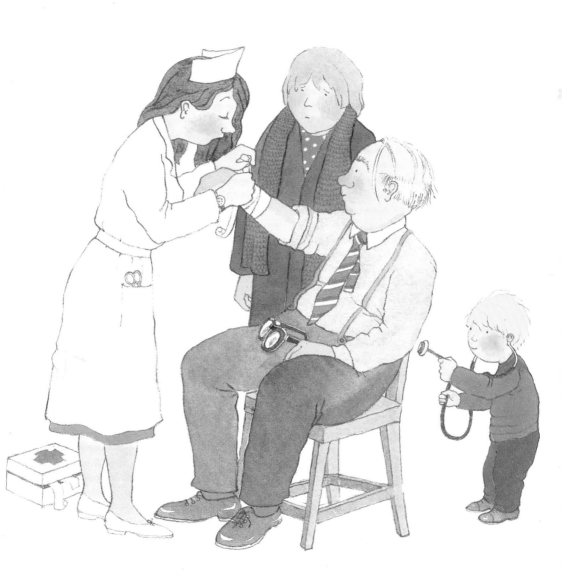

'He seems normal enough,'
the doctor said. 'I won't
need to see him again for
some time, I hope.'
'I like the doctor,' I said.
'I think he's really nice.'